This Book Belongs to:

Mickey's
Young Readers Library

VOLUME

2

Donald's Big News

© MCMXC **The Walt Disney Company.**
Developed by The Walt Disney Company in conjunction with Nancy Hall, Inc.
Story by Mary Packard/Activities by Thoburn Educational Enterprises, Inc.
This book may not be reproduced or transmitted in any form or by any means.
ISBN 1-885222-35-1
Advance Publishers Inc., P.O. Box 2607, Winter Park, FL. 32790
Printed in the United States of America
0987654321

One day, Donald walked up the path to Grandma Duck's house. He was about to ring the doorbell when he overheard Grandma say, "Oh, dear, I'm afraid I've lost it! And it's been in the family forever! What will I do? What will we eat?"

"Poor Grandma," Donald thought. "She sounds so upset!"

Donald sat down on the porch steps to think.
What could Grandma have lost?

"Could it be her favorite hat?" Donald wondered.
"But, no, she said, 'What will we eat?' You can't eat
a hat. Besides, Grandma gets all our food from the
farm. Hmmmm, what is something that has been in
the family for years?"

Then it came to him! "The farm!" he cried. "Oh,
no! Grandma is losing the farm!"

"This is terrible," he moaned. "What are we going to do?"

Donald hurried away from Grandma's house. Over and over again, he kept saying, "This is terrible—just terrible!"

Donald was so upset that he didn't see Huey, Dewey, and Louie.

"Gee, Uncle Donald, you almost knocked us over," Huey told him.

"We've got a big problem!" Donald told them. "Something awful! Something terrible!"

"Something terrible?" Dewey repeated. "What do you mean?"

Donald explained about Grandma losing the farm and not having anything to eat.

"This really is a problem," the nephews agreed.

"What are we going to do?" Donald asked.

"We could ask Uncle Scrooge. Maybe he would give Grandma the money," Dewey said.

"Are you kidding?" Huey asked. "Uncle Scrooge doesn't give money away. We have to think of a plan of our own!"

"I know!" Huey said. "We could sell lemonade."

"Lemonade!" said Louie. "We could never sell enough lemonade to save Grandma's farm!"

"Well, then," said Huey, "you come up with an idea."

"I've got it!" shouted Louie. "Let's hold a yard sale for Grandma. With the money we make, we can save the farm."

"Great idea!" agreed Donald.

The three nephews jumped into action. They left
Donald to spread the word about the yard sale.

Huey, Dewey, and Louie hurried to their basement. They gathered up their old toys: a worn baseball, a tennis ball, some old books, and other things like that. They piled them all into a wagon. Then they headed for Grandma's yard.

"Save the farm!" they shouted. "Save the farm!"
Soon all of Duckburg knew about Grandma Duck's
problem and the yard sale at her farm.

Every person promised to come to the yard sale.
They would bring some of their old things to sell.
And they promised to buy other people's old things,
so they could help Grandma Duck save her farm.

Gyro Gearloose had just finished building his latest invention, a super-duper printing press. Then he heard the noise in the street.

When he learned about Donald's big news,
Gyro used his super-duper printing press to print up
a grand banner so everyone would know what the
yard sale was about.

Gus Goose was just about to take his second
nap of the day. Then he heard the shout outside,
"Save the farm! Save the farm!"

"Fuss and feathers!" grumbled the lazy goose, sticking his head out the window. "What's going on?" he asked.

"Grandma's going to lose her farm," said Donald. "We're having a yard sale to help her."

"Losing Grandma's farm would be awful," Gus decided with a yawn. "Maybe I should go and have a look."

So Gus gathered a few of the things he thought he might need. He took his quilt, his hammock, and his favorite, softest pillow. Who knew how long he might be gone? And he didn't want to miss his next nap!

Daisy was busy baking apple pies when she heard the crowd go by. "Save the farm!" they shouted. "Save the farm!"

Daisy stuck her head out the window and read Gyro's banner.

"Grandma in trouble? How dreadful!" Daisy cried. "But maybe I can help. Surely someone will buy some pie."

Then she joined the crowd, carrying a tall stack of pies.

Gladstone Gander was walking down the street
when he noticed everyone hurrying toward
Grandma Duck's house.
   "Save Grandma Duck's farm!" Gladstone heard
Donald say.

"Grandma Duck about to lose her farm! Oh, my!
I'd better hurry over there right this minute. It sounds
like she could use a little luck, and I'm the good-luck
gander if ever there was one!" Gladstone said. Then
he, too, joined the crowd headed for Grandma
Duck's farm.

As the crowd continued on to Grandma Duck's farm, Uncle Scrooge walked by.

"Oh, Uncle Scrooge," said Donald, "thank goodness you're here! Something terrible is happening."

"What is it?" asked Uncle Scrooge.

"Well, Grandma's run out of money, and she's losing the farm. She has nothing to eat, and we're having a yard sale, and . . ." Donald began.

"Say no more, my boy! There's not a minute to lose! Then he dug deep into his pocket. He pulled out a roll of bills. "When your yard sale is over," said Scrooge, "tell me how much money you've raised, and I'll match it!"

Donald and the others were glad that Uncle Scrooge was willing to help. Happily they all set out again for the yard sale. Huey, Dewey, and Louie hung Gyro's huge banner, which said "SAVE GRANDMA'S FARM" in great big letters.

Daisy filled a table with the delicious pies she'd brought.

And all the families from miles around came to the sale. Some brought old pots and pans, books and boxes. Some brought old dresses, hats, pants, and even shoes! Everyone brought something to sell. And everyone looked around eagerly for something to buy.

Suddenly Grandma came out on the porch.
"What's all this noise?" she asked. "What's
going on?"

"Don't worry, Grandma," Donald said. "Your
problems are over."

"What problems, Donald?" Grandma asked.
Then she looked around. She noticed all the people
in her yard.

"Why are all these people here?" she asked.
Just then the crowd grew quiet. Everyone gathered round to listen.

"Well, you see," Donald began, "this morning I heard you say you had lost something that had been in the family for years. I knew you meant the farm," he explained, "so we all decided to help you save it."

"I see . . . I think," Grandma said slowly. "So all these good people are here because they want to help you save my farm?"

"That's right, Grandma," said Donald. "We're holding a yard sale to raise the money," Donald said with a proud smile.

"But, I didn't lose my farm," said Grandma.

"Then what did you lose?" asked Donald.

"Silly Donald," said Grandma, shaking her head. "What I lost was my apple-pie recipe."

Before Donald could say anything at all, Daisy spoke up. "Why, Grandma, I borrowed that recipe from you just the other day. I used it to make all these pies."

Everyone looked from the pies to Donald. He was embarrassed.

"I'm sorry, Grandma," said Donald. "I guess I should have found out all the facts before I made such a fuss."

Grandma knew how Donald was feeling. "It's all right, Donald," she said. "I know you meant well. Besides, you showed me something very special today."

"What's that, Grandma?" Donald asked.

"You showed me how much my family and neighbors care about me," she said with a smile.

Everyone cheered for Grandma. Then she said, "Why don't you start cutting those pies, Daisy? I'll make some of my special lemonade. We can have a party instead of a yard sale—in honor of all of you!"

Think About It

The Main Idea

Read the sentences below. Which one best describes the lesson Donald learned in the story you've just read? Why? Explain why the other sentences don't describe what Donald learned.

1. If you have a lot of old things, it's a good idea to have a yard sale.
2. Don't spread news of disaster until you have all the facts.
3. Keep track of other people's recipes because you never know when they'll need them.

After your child does the activities in this book, refer to the *Young Readers Guide* for the answers to these activities and for additional games, activities, and ideas.

Match It Up

Do you remember who brought what to the yard sale? Match the characters on the left to the things they brought.

SAVE GRANDMA'S FARM

yard-sale banner

apple pies

old games and toys

wad of bills

hammock & pillow

Fun With Words

Your Yard Sale

If you were going to have a yard sale to raise money, what things would you bring? (Use the items shown below to help you start off your list.)

What Did Grandma Lose?

Do you remember what Grandma lost? To find out, follow the path of things in the order that they were taken to the yard sale.

SAVE GRANDMA'S FARM

RECIPE

ckey's Young Readers Library • Mickey's Young Readers Library • Mickey's Yo
ung Readers Library • Mickey's Young Readers Library • Mickey's Young Reac
Mickey's Young Readers Library • Mick